A WOLF at the DOOR!

Nick Ward

For Rob O'Connor

Scholastic Children's Books,
Commonwealth House, 1-19 New Oxford Street,
London WC1A 1NU, UK
a division of Scholastic Ltd

London ~ New York ~ Toronto ~ Sydney ~ Auckland
Mexico City ~ New Delhi ~ Hong Kong

First published by Scholastic Ltd, 2001

One quiet afternoon, while Father Bear
was in the yard chopping wood, Little
Bear sat reading his favourite book.
All was cosy and peaceful, when . . .

Knock! Knock! went the door.
"Who's there?" asked Little Bear,
jumping down from his chair.

"It's Billy," a tiny voice bleated. "Please let me in." Little Bear lifted the latch, opened the door and in trotted . . .

. . . Little Billy Goat Gruff! "Lock the door, quickly!" bleated Billy. "A wolf is after me! And he shouted, 'Come out, come out, wherever you are!'"

"I saw him up on the mountain," the little goat whimpered. "I saw his long, black shadow. He looked lean and mean, so I ran and ran 'til I got to your door!"

Little Bear sat Billy down.
"Don't worry," he said. "You're safe here."
And he started to read Billy a story.
All was cosy and quiet, when . . .

KNOCK! KNOCK!
went the door!
"Who's there?" called Little Bear.
"It's the Squealer Boys!
Please let us in."

Little Bear lifted the
latch, opened
the door and in trotted . . .

. . . the three little pigs!
"Lock the door, quickly!" they cried.
"A huge wolf is after us! He came
to our house and he roared,
'Come out, come out, wherever you
are!' He was fierce. He was angry!"
"And he was lean and mean,"
added Billy.

"We left our house and ran
and ran, 'til we got to your
door," squealed
the three pigs.

Little Bear let
them in and
locked the door.

"Don't worry," said Little Bear.
"You're safe here." And he sat them
down to listen to the story. All was
quiet and calm, when . . .

KNOCK! KNOCK!

went the door!
"Who's there?" called Little Bear.
"It's Bo," said a voice.
"Please let me in."

Little Bear lifted
the latch, opened
the door and
in rushed . . .

. . . Little Bo Peep and all her sheep!

"Lock the door," cried Bo Peep. "A wolf is after us!"

"What happened?" asked Little Bear, as he locked the door, quickly.

"Down in the field," panted Bo Peep. "I heard the hedge rustle and I saw his bushy tail. And he bellowed . . ."

"We ran for our lives," chorused the
sheep. "But he chased us!"
"We could hear him panting."
"We could feel his hot, wolfie breath."
"He was huge," baaed the sheep.
"He was fierce and angry," piped
the pigs.
"He was lean and mean," bleated Billy.
"And we didn't stop 'til we got to your
door," finished Bo Peep.

So Little Bear sat them all down and started to read his story. But he kept being interrupted by a **Knock! Knock!** at the door.

First there was Little Red Riding Hood,

then Cinderella,

and finally Goldilocks.

They had all come to hide from the wicked wolf. "Don't worry," Little Bear told them. "You are all safe here."

Father Bear came in from the yard. "Goodness," he gasped. "What are all your friends doing here?"

"They've escaped from a terrible wolf," said Little Bear.

Just then, **KNOCK! KNOCK!** went the door. The house . . . went . . . very . . . very . . . quiet.

Father Bear slowly
unlocked the door.
"Who's there?" he boomed. . . .

They all went out and played 'til bedtime!
"That was fun!" said Wolfie afterwards.
"Come again soon!" said Little Bear.